Smuggler's Cave

Sonya Spreen Bates

Illustrated by Kasia Charko

ORCA BOOK PUBLISHERS

Library and Archives Canada Cataloguing in Publication

Bates, Sonya Spreen
Smuggler's cave / written by Sonya Spreen Bates ; illustrated by Kasia Charko.
(Orca echoes)

Issued also in an electronic format.
ISBN 978-1-55469-308-5

I. Charko, Kasia, 1949- II. Title. III. Series: Orca echoes.
PS8603.A846S68 2010   JC813'.6   C2010-903525-9

First published in the United States, 2010
Library of Congress Control Number: 2010928736

Summary: Jake and Tommy find themselves back on Marsh Island,
but this time they're trapped in a sea cave with their cousin Lexie.

Orca Book Publishers gratefully acknowledges the support for its publishing programs
provided by the following agencies: the Government of Canada through the Canada Book
Fund and the Canada Council for the Arts, and the Province of British Columbia
through the BC Arts Council and the Book Publishing Tax Credit.

Mixed Sources
Cert no. SW-COC-001271
© 1996 FSC
FSC

*Orca Book Publishers is dedicated to preserving the environment and has printed this book
on paper certified by the Forest Stewardship Council.*

Typesetting by Teresa Bubela
Cover artwork and interior illustrations by Kasia Charko

ORCA BOOK PUBLISHERS   ORCA BOOK PUBLISHERS
PO BOX 5626, STN. B   PO BOX 468
VICTORIA, BC CANADA   CUSTER, WA USA
V8R 6S4   98240-0468

www.orcabook.com
Printed and bound in Canada.

13 12 11 10 • 4 3 2 1

For Dad, with love.

Chapter One
THE RACE

Jake hopped off his bike. He dropped it on the grass at the top of the cliff and started down the steps to the beach. His feet pounded on the wooden planks. The wind was cold on his cheeks. He could smell the salty seaweed scent of the ocean.

I am a triathlete, he thought. *Fast, strong and powerful. I finished the bicycle race and am in the lead. No one will catch me.*

He heard the thud of footsteps behind him. Glancing back, he saw Lexie, his cousin, starting down the stairs.

A competitor! Jake thought. *I cannot let her pass.* He picked up the pace.

The beach was a long way down. One hundred and thirty steps. He had counted them the day before when he arrived at the beach house with Mom and Dad and his brother Tommy. Aunt Bonnie and Uncle Max rented the house every Thanksgiving. This was the first time Jake and his family had been there.

Jake knew Lexie was fast. He'd raced her before, lots of times. He wasn't going to let her win.

Gripping the handrail, Jake swung past the bend in the stairs. He was halfway down. His legs hurt like crazy, and he was huffing and puffing like a steam train.

"JAKE!" The scream came from the top of the stairs. "Jake, wait for me!"

It was Tommy, Jake's younger brother, coming last as usual. Jake glanced back up the stairs, and that's when it happened. He missed a step.

He felt himself falling and grabbed for the rail. Lexie raced past him.

"Yes!" she cried.

Jake tore after her.

It's a race for gold, he thought. *I must go faster.* The stairs were a blur. Faster and faster he went, down, down, down toward the beach. He jumped the last few steps, landing in the sand only a second behind Lexie.

"I win! I win!" she shouted, jumping around and pumping her fists in the air. Her curly brown ponytail bounced wildly. "I win and you lose!" Lexie was small for her age. Even though she was ten and Jake was still nine, she was shorter than him by four or five centimeters. She was almost as small as Tommy.

Jake unzipped his hoodie and bent over, trying to catch his breath. "You only won because I tripped. I had you beat, easy."

"No way," said Lexie, shaking her head. "I beat you fair and square. I'm the winner. Again." She danced a little jig.

Jake didn't say anything. Lexie would be gloating all day. She always did. Last Christmas they'd had a toboggan race down the hill behind Jake's house. Lexie won by half a sled. She bragged about it all afternoon and made herself a trophy in the snow.

"Jake!" Tommy's voice came from halfway down the stairs. "Wait up! Mom said we have to stick together!"

Jake glared at his brother. If it wasn't for Tommy, he would have won the race. Tommy was always spoiling things.

"Hurry up then, slowpoke," he called, "or I'll tell Mom you didn't stick with us like you were supposed to."

"But Jake—," said Tommy.

"Ah, leave him alone," said Lexie. When Tommy reached the bottom of the stairs, she pulled a long blue ribbon out of her pocket and threaded it through a shell. "Here, Tommy, you can present the gold medal."

Lexie's pockets were always filled with stuff: bits of string, a pocketknife, rubber bands, paper clips, stubby pencils or chalk. One time, when they needed to get a key out of a drain, she had found a magnet in her back pocket.

Tommy placed the ribbon around her neck. Lexie bowed to the seagulls strutting on the beach. "Thank you, thank you," she said.

"You are so full of it," said Jake, shaking his head.

"You're just mad because you lost," said Lexie.

"I am not," said Jake. He pushed the hair off his face. Tommy's hair was curly like Lexie's, but Jake's was straight and always seemed to get in his eyes.

"You are too," said Lexie in a smug voice. "I won, and you can't stand it."

"I can beat you anytime I want," said Jake. He picked up a stone and threw it into the waves.

"So prove it," said Lexie.

Jake turned to look at her. She was wearing shorts and a sweatshirt, even though it was October and the wind was quite cold. Jake stuck his hands in the pockets of his jeans.

"How?" he asked.

"Another race," she said, grinning. "A boat race." She pointed toward four small rowboats lined up on the sand at the edge of the water.

Jake liked boats. He was a good rower. His dad taught him how to row when they went camping last summer. His dad had taught him lots of things—how to use a compass, how to start a campfire and how to roast marshmallows without burning them. "All right," Jake said. "To the end of the beach and back?"

Lexie shook her head, making her ponytail bounce back and forth again. "Nah, too easy. To the island."

Jake's eyes swiveled round to the small island about five hundred meters offshore.

"You mean Marsh Island?" said Tommy in a hushed voice.

"Of course," said Lexie. "Do you see any other islands around here?"

Jake and Tommy exchanged glances. Last summer, they had camped with their dad on Marsh Island. Strange things happened there.

"Sure," said Jake, eyeing the calm stretch of sea between the beach and the island. "I could make that, easy."

"All the way round the other side?" said Lexie.

"There's no beach on the other side of the island," said Jake.

"We're not going to the beach," said Lexie. "We're going to Smuggler's Cave."

Chapter Two
DISASTER

"Smuggler's Cave?" said Tommy. "What's that?"

"You haven't heard of Smuggler's Cave?" said Lexie.

Tommy shook his head.

Jake had. He remembered hearing about Smuggler's Cave from Chris Mumford, the man from the Marsh Island Historical Society who took care of the island.

"It's a cave on the other side of the island," said Lexie. "Smugglers used to stash their loot there. That's why it's called Smuggler's Cave."

"What kind of loot?" asked Jake.

"All sorts. Tea, wine, silks, spices—even money and pirate treasure." Her eyes gleamed. "It's the perfect hiding spot. The only way in is by boat, and only at low tide."

"Why only at low tide?" asked Tommy.

"Because," said Lexie, "when the water rises, the cave fills until the entrance is underwater. No one can get in, and no one can get out."

Jake stared at the island. He imagined what it would be like hiding in the cave, alone in the dark, surrounded by stolen treasure, waiting for a ship to come. He shivered.

"So," said Lexie, "are we gonna race?"

"Don't do it, Jake," said Tommy, tugging at Jake's sleeve. "That island is creepy."

Jake had never rowed that far from the beach. And he had to admit, there was something weird about Marsh Island.

"You're chicken," said Lexie.

"I'm not chicken," said Jake.

Lexie started flapping her arms and clucking like a hen.

Jake scowled at her. "Fine, let's race then," he said. "Come on, Tommy. We'll take the red boat."

Lexie let out a whoop of triumph. She raced for the boats.

"Me?" said Tommy. "Why do I have to come?"

"Because," said Jake, "there's no way I'm leaving you here on the beach by yourself. Mom would kill me."

He shoved Tommy into the back of the boat, tossed him a life jacket and jammed another one over his own head.

Lexie tightened the strap on her life jacket and grinned. "First one to Smuggler's Cave wins."

Jake pushed the boat off the sand and hopped on board. Grabbing the oars, he struggled to get them into position. Lexie was already rowing toward the island.

"Hurry, Jake," said Tommy. "She's beating us."

"I know," said Jake. "Be quiet now so I can concentrate."

Finally he got the oars into the water. He dipped them deep and pulled hard. The boat was heavy. It took a while to get going, but soon he was into a rhythm. Dip and pull, dip and pull.

"Faster, Jake, faster," said Tommy.

It felt good being out on the water. The wind was cold. Now and then a spray of salt water splashed over him. The waves were bigger than he had thought. The sea wasn't as calm as it had looked from shore. The boat rocked back and forth with each pull of the oars. Jake watched as the beach moved farther and farther away. It made him a bit uneasy. He glanced behind him. Lexie was only a couple of meters ahead. Marsh Island still seemed a long way away.

I am an Olympic rower, thought Jake. *I glide through the water, strong and silent as a shark. My opponent is only meters ahead of me. With each stroke I come closer to winning a gold medal.*

Dip and pull. Dip and pull. Jake's arms started to ache.

"Come on, you're gaining on her," said Tommy, bouncing in his seat. The life jacket was huge on him. With his arms and head sticking out of the holes, he looked like a turtle bouncing around in its shell.

"Sit still!" said Jake. "You're rocking the boat."

Dip and pull. Dip and pull. Slowly they caught up to Lexie. The two boats were right alongside each other. Lexie grinned at Jake.

"Give up!" said Jake. "You're done for!"

"No way!" Lexie called back. She pulled harder on her oars and moved ahead.

"Faster, Jake, she's beating us!" said Tommy.

Jake leaned into the oars. His whole body hurt, and he was breathing like a racehorse. He made himself go faster. Back and forth. Dip and pull. He couldn't let Lexie win. Not this time. Not when he was so close.

They were moving around the island now. Jake could see it off to his right. Lexie was on his left.

As he glanced over at her, their oars clashed and the wooden handle almost slipped out of his hand. He gripped harder and kept rowing.

"I can see the cave. We're almost there!" said Tommy.

Jake looked over his shoulder toward Marsh Island. Ahead of him was a sheer cliff. Huge boulders stuck out of the water below it. In the middle of the cliff was a dark opening—Smuggler's Cave.

Jake felt a surge of energy. He was going to do it. He was going to beat Lexie. He pulled harder. Slowly their boat moved ahead.

The sea was rougher on this side of the island. Waves splashed over the side of the boat, making a puddle on the bottom. The tide was stronger too. It pushed them toward the island, toward the cliff. He struggled to keep the boat straight, pulling hard with his right oar.

Lexie was behind him. She steered her boat farther out to sea and shouted something to him. Jake couldn't make out what she said.

The cliff was only meters away. Jake dragged the oars through the water.

"Watch out for the rocks, Jake," said Tommy. "You're getting too close."

"I know," said Jake. "I'm trying."

The boat was pushed closer to the cliff with each surge of the sea. Jake glanced back and saw the entrance to the cave a short distance away. Each time a wave hit, water rushed into the hole, like storm water down a drain. Then it was sucked out again as the wave receded.

"Jake! Look out!" said Tommy, standing up and pointing.

Jake saw the cliff loom up in front of him. "Hold on!" he shouted.

The boat smashed into the rock. It hit with a *CRACK* and rocked sideways. Jake clung to the sides of the boat. Tommy threw his arms up, trying to get his balance. Then there was a *SPLASH*. Tommy had fallen overboard.

Chapter Three
BOY OVERBOARD

Jake saw Tommy plunge into the water and quickly bob up again. The life jacket kept him afloat, but waves splashed over his face. He flailed his arms around, coughing and spluttering.

"Help!" Tommy screamed. "Help!"

Jake leaned over the edge of the boat. He stretched an arm toward Tommy. "Grab my hand!" he called.

Tommy threw his arms around wildly. His fingers brushed Jake's hand. But Jake couldn't catch hold of them.

"Over here, Tommy!" said Jake. "Grab my hand." He stretched farther over the edge of the boat. The boat rocked dangerously.

Tommy turned and saw Jake's hand. He made a grab for it. Jake's fingers closed over Tommy's. He had him!

Another big wave hit the boat, and it smashed up against the rocks. Jake felt himself falling. Before he knew what was happening, he was in the water too.

Jake's mouth filled with water. Everything was dark and murky. He didn't know which way was up. He kicked his legs as the life jacket brought him to the surface. He came up gasping for air.

The boat was a couple of meters away. It had overturned and was floating upside down. Tommy was bobbing next to it.

Jake swam toward the boat. Grabbing on to it with one hand, he took hold of the back of Tommy's life jacket with the other.

"Jake!" said Tommy. "I thought you had drowned."

"Of course I didn't drown," said Jake. He tried to make his voice sound like he wasn't scared. "Here, hang on to the boat."

The sea tossed them up and down with the waves. Jake clung tightly to the keel of the boat. He didn't know how long he could hang on. His legs felt like dead weights, and he couldn't catch his breath. The water was cold. Really cold. He knew they should try to flip the boat over, but he was too tired.

The boat bumped and bobbed against the rocks. The surging waves threw it against the cliff and then drew it back again, taking Jake and Tommy with it. Jake looked up and saw the entrance to the cave only a couple of meters away. Suddenly he realized what was happening. The current was going to take them right into Smuggler's Cave.

"Hold on, Tommy," he cried.

The next wave sent them rushing through the low narrow opening. Tommy screamed as they were swept into the dark hole. Jake held on to him tightly. The boat pitched wildly as the swell dragged them back and then threw them forward, farther into the cave.

Light streamed into the cave's mouth. The cave was big, long and narrow. Jake could see the roof of the cavern above them. The walls rose steeply out of the water, with rocks and ledges near the water's edge. Jake heard the sound of water lapping on the cave walls and waves breaking against the rocks.

"Where are we?" whispered Tommy.

"We're in Smuggler's Cave," said Jake.

Tommy looked around fearfully. "Are there smugglers in here?"

"No," said Jake. "That was ages ago."

A wave pushed them farther into the cave. The swell was smaller now that they were away from the entrance. The deeper they went, the darker it got. Jake started to panic. They would drift forever and get trapped in the dark. No one would ever find them—like being shipwrecked on a deserted island.

Jake knew they had to get out of the water. "Help me," he said. "Kick your legs."

Together they pushed the boat toward a low ledge. When it bumped up against the rock, they scrambled out of the water and flopped onto the ground. It smelled salty and fishy in the cave. Jake rolled over, and his hand splashed into water. Sitting up, he saw a tide pool filled with starfish.

Tommy pushed himself up. "Jake, the boat!" he said.

Jake spun around. The boat was several meters away, moving slowly toward the back of the cave. He groaned.

"What are we going to do now?" asked Tommy.

"I—I don't know," said Jake, glancing down at his brother.

Tommy's eyes were big and round. His bottom lip trembled.

Jake put a hand on Tommy's shoulder, just like Dad did to calm them down. "It's all right," Jake said. "Lexie will go and get help. We'll just wait here until someone—"

A scream tore through the air, echoing around the cave.

Jake jumped. Lexie's boat shot through the entrance of the cave, riding in on a wave like a surfboard.

"Jake! Tommy! Where are you?" called Lexie.

"Over here!" Jake said.

Lexie spotted them and rowed toward the ledge.

"What are you doing here?" said Jake when she reached them.

"Rescuing you, of course," said Lexie. "Hop in."

"Hurray!" said Tommy.

Jake wasn't so sure. The tide looked like it was rising. He remembered what Lexie had said about the tide. If they hurried, they might make it out in time. But if they didn't…No one knew where they were. No one would ever think to look for them in Smuggler's Cave.

The boys scrambled into the boat, and Lexie turned the bow toward the cave's mouth. It was slow going. Lexie was small, and the boat was heavy with the three of them in it. She rowed hard, a determined look on her face. As they got closer to the entrance of the cave, each surge of water pushed them back. It was as if the sea was trying to prevent them from escaping.

Jake glanced toward the entrance. It wasn't getting any closer. And the opening looked smaller than before. The tide was definitely rising.

"Here, let me row," said Jake, reaching for the oars.

"I can do it," said Lexie through gritted teeth.

"Don't be stupid. I'm stronger than you," said Jake. "I'll get us out faster."

"No!" said Lexie.

Tommy looked scared. "Come on, Lexie. Let Jake help. We have to get out," he said.

Lexie paused in her rowing. "All right," she said. "Take one of the oars. It'll be faster if we both row."

Jake scooted over next to her. His heart was beating as fast as a fighter jet. They had to get out. And soon.

Together they leaned forward, dipped the oars and pulled. Dip and pull, dip and pull.

I am a slave on an ancient warship, thought Jake. *I row with my fellow slaves. Day after day we row. We don't know where we're going. We don't know when we will reach land. We just row.*

"You're doing it!" cried Tommy. "We're getting closer."

The sea is strong. The master calls for more power, Jake thought. He didn't dare look back. He kept his eyes down and rowed with all his might. The tide pulled them forward and then threw them back again. Water splashed over the sides of the boat. It sprayed in Jake's face. His lips tasted salty.

"Almost there!" said Tommy. "Over to the right a bit. You're getting too close to the wall."

Jake was pulling too hard. Lexie wasn't as strong as him. He was making them go off-course.

Suddenly there was a loud *CRACK*. Lexie cried out and dropped her oar. As Jake pulled, the boat

turned sideways and hit the wall. A wave crashed through the opening, and they were swept back into the cave. With only one oar, they watched helplessly as the waves pushed them past the ledge where they had been sitting and into the darkness beyond.

Chapter Four
SMUGGLER'S CAVE

Everything was dark. Jake heard a strange moaning sound. It sounded like a ghost or a zombie or something. "Tommy, quit making that noise," Jake said.

The noise stopped. Tommy sniffed and hiccupped. "Jake, I'm scared," he said.

"I know," said Jake. "Now be quiet so I can think."

Lexie dug in her pocket. She snapped on a small flashlight. "Think about what?" she said. "How you can get us into more trouble?"

"Me!" said Jake. "It's not my fault. You're the one who dropped your oar."

"Only because we ran into the wall. You couldn't even steer straight," she said.

"Well, if you'd just gone to get help instead of trying to be a hero, we wouldn't be in this mess," said Jake.

Lexie glared at him. "And you and Tommy would still be sitting on that ledge."

"Shut up!" cried Tommy, covering his ears.

Jake and Lexie both turned to look at him. Tommy's face was white in the pale light. He was shivering.

"Sorry," Jake said. "You're right. We should be trying to figure out how to get out of here."

"How are we gonna get out with only one oar?" Lexie whispered so Tommy couldn't hear. "Besides, I told you, once the tide comes in we'll be trapped."

"Well, we've gotta try," said Jake.

He seized the flashlight from Lexie and shone it into the darkness. The cave seemed to go on forever. Jake heard water lapping at the cave walls. The air smelled damp and salty.

"What's that up there?" said Lexie.

Up ahead, something strange gleamed in the darkness. They drifted to the back of the cave. A small sandy beach sloped up toward a rocky platform about the size of Jake and Tommy's backyard.

The boat bumped against the sand with a gritty scraping sound. Jake and Tommy's boat was already there, stuck in the sand.

"This must be where the smugglers stored their loot," said Lexie. She chucked her life jacket on the bottom of the boat and climbed out.

Tommy grabbed Jake's arm as Jake dragged his own life jacket over his head. "Don't leave me here by myself," Tommy said.

"Come on then," said Jake.

Tommy tossed his jacket on the floor with the others and scrambled out of the boat after Jake.

Jake moved toward the back of the cave. Tommy clung to his sleeve. A line of shells and seaweed

about a meter up from the water's edge marked the high-tide line. Farther back the rocky platform sloped up into the darkness.

"Jake, over here," called Lexie.

Jake flashed the light in her direction. She was standing on a ledge. There were rock ledges and crevices all over the back of the cave. He climbed up next to her and shone the flashlight on a small mound of white sticks.

The sticks were all sorts of shapes. Some were long and thick, some were small and straight, some curved, some knobby. As Lexie reached down to touch one, Jake's scalp started to prickle. "Don't touch them!" he said.

Lexie jumped back.

"Those are bones," he said.

Tommy peered out from behind him. "Human bones?"

"Could be," said Jake, eyeing them warily. "Maybe it's one of the smugglers." *How long have these been here?* thought Jake. *A hundred years? Two hundred?*

Lexie glared at Jake but didn't touch them. "As if," she said. "They're probably just animal bones."

The bones made Jake's stomach queasy. He didn't like being near them. He moved away and Tommy and Lexie followed close behind.

Jake walked along the ledge, deeper into the cave. He couldn't tell how far it went. He shone the flashlight on the floor, the walls and up on the ceiling. He had a strange feeling. Like there was something in the cave with them. *Were those really the bones of a smuggler?* he wondered. *Maybe one who was trapped in the cave and never got out?*

"Let's go back to the boats," said Tommy. "This place is creepy."

"Not yet," said Jake. "I want to have a look around." He didn't tell Tommy the boats couldn't help them anymore. The mouth of the cave was already underwater.

Lexie pointed at the ceiling. "What was that?" she whispered. "I thought I saw something."

Jake saw a shadow move. Suddenly there was an ear-splitting screech. He dropped the flashlight, and they all covered their ears with their hands. The air was alive.

Chapter Five
TRAPPED

Hundreds of tiny furry bodies flew past them, brushed against their faces and careened into their heads and shoulders. The air was filled with a high-pitched squealing. Bats!

Jake flailed his arms, trying to hit the creatures away. His heart was banging against his ribs.

"Ahh! Ahh!" cried Tommy. "Get away from me!" He spun around, stumbling to get away from the bats.

"There's one in my hair!" screeched Lexie. She whipped her head around to get rid of it.

"Stand still!" Jake said. "Hold still and they won't fly into you."

"I can't! Get them away!" said Tommy. Jake could hear the fear in his voice. He was feeling panicked too.

Tommy's voice rose to a shriek. Jake heard a *THUMP*.

"Tommy!" Jake said. He reached out to grab him, but he wasn't there.

The bats streamed toward the back of the cave. They flew up toward the ceiling and disappeared. All was quiet. The flashlight lay on the ground where Jake had dropped it. Heart still pounding, he picked it up.

"Tommy?" Jake said. "Tommy! Where are you?"

"Down here." Tommy's voice was small and scared.

Jake and Lexie knelt on the rock and shone the flashlight over the edge. Tommy sat at the bottom, clutching his ankle.

"Are you all right?" Jake called down.

"No," said Tommy. Jake could tell he was trying not to cry. "My foot hurts really bad."

Jake and Lexie climbed down to where Tommy lay on the beach. Jake had a bad feeling in his stomach again. Tommy had fallen off the ledge. He was hurt. And no one knew where they were.

"Just stay still. I'm going to get help," said Jake.

"Don't leave me here!" cried Tommy.

Lexie rolled her eyes. "How are you gonna get help? Swim? Underwater?"

"Listen," said Jake. "Those bats went somewhere. There must be another way out."

"That's crazy," Lexie said, but Jake could tell she was thinking about it.

"It's worth a try," he said.

Tommy struggled to his feet, balancing on one foot. "I'm coming too."

"Don't be silly, Tommy. You're hurt," said Jake.

Tommy's lip trembled. "I'm not staying here in the dark."

"He's right," said Lexie. "We should stick together. If you go, we all go."

Jake glanced at Tommy. "All right. Let's go then," Jake said. "But no whining."

Jake led the way, clambering up the rocks and along the ledges toward the back of the cave to where he had seen the bats disappear. It was slow going. Tommy couldn't put much weight on his foot, so they had to help him.

I am the leader of an expedition, Jake thought. *I am fearless and brave. I search for an escape.*

The ground sloped steeply up toward the ceiling. The walls were covered in white paste from water that seeped from the rocks. Jake looked back. It was like they were climbing to the top of a cliff. He flashed the light around, looking for where the bats had gone. Up ahead, the cave seemed to come to an end. There had to be a way out.

"What's that up there?" said Lexie.

Jake shone the light in the direction she was pointing. He didn't see anything at first. Then he spotted it. A crevice in the rock.

"That's it!" said Jake.

They scrambled across the rocks. The crack in the wall was perfect for bats and just big enough for a person to squeeze through. Jake shone the light inside. All he saw was darkness.

"I don't think we should go in there," said Tommy. "Let's go back."

"No way, Tommy. We're not going back," said Jake. "The bats got out this way, and so can we."

He ducked his head and slipped through the hole. Inside was a smaller cave. It smelled rank and musky, a bit like an outhouse. Water dripped down the walls. A few small stalactites hung from the ceiling like icicles. There was something squishy under his feet. He wrinkled his nose.

Lexie and Tommy came through the crack.

"What's that smell?" said Tommy.

"Bat pooh," said Jake.

"Ewww." Tommy covered his nose.

Did the smugglers come this way? Jake wondered. *Did they search for an escape route too?*

Looking closer, he saw there was something on the wall. A figure of a man. A man with a spear and a large animal with sharp horns. Cave drawings!

"Look at this," he said.

"That is so cool," said Lexie.

There were other drawings as well: all sorts of animals, more men hunting, men at war. They showed life as it was thousands of years ago. Life before there were cars and telephones and computers, and even things like shops and money. Life when the only rule was hunt or be hunted.

A cold draft blew across Jake's face. He looked up. A sliver of light shone through a hole above them.

"Look," he said triumphantly. "That's our way out."

The hole was up high, at the top of a small narrow shaft. It looked like a chimney. Bats could easily escape through it, and small creatures like rats

and rabbits, or even raccoons. But not smugglers. They could never have escaped this way.

Are we small enough to fit through? thought Jake. *There's only one way to find out.* He clambered up onto a ledge. He put one foot on a rock, reached as high as he could and found a handhold on the wall. Gripping tight with his fingers, he pulled himself up.

It's like the rock-climbing wall at the park at home, he told himself. But the wall at home wasn't this big. It wasn't wet and slippery. And there was nice soft grass at the bottom, not solid rock. Jake felt his fingers slipping. He dug his toes into the wall, just like his dad had taught him. He wished Dad were here now. He tried to get a better grip with his fingers, but he couldn't hold on and dropped back onto the ledge.

"It's too high. The wall's too slippery," he said.

"Let me try," said Lexie, climbing up next to him.

"You won't be able to reach," said Jake. "You're even smaller than me."

"I will if you give me a boost," she said.

Jake had to admit it was a good idea. He cupped his hand under Lexie's foot and lifted her up.

She reached for the gap at the top. "I'm almost there. Just a little bit higher," she said.

Jake boosted her up as high as he could.

"Got it!" she said. She pulled herself up.

Jake watched her legs kicking about as she heaved herself through the hole. Then her legs and feet disappeared. "I'm out," she said.

"Hurray!" said Tommy.

Lexie popped her head back through the hole. "Now it's your turn, Tommy."

Jake gave Tommy a boost. Lexie reached down and grabbed his hands. She hauled him up, and Tommy scrambled out.

Jake looked up. Lexie was reaching toward him. She looked so small and the opening was so high. Would she be able to pull him through?

"Come on, Jake," said Lexie. "Don't be a wuss."

Jake glared at her. He wasn't a wuss.

He reached up and wedged his fingers over the rock. He dug his toes into the wall and grabbed for Lexie's hand. He felt her fingers clamp down on his. Her other hand went around his wrist. She was stronger than he'd thought. He pushed with his legs and got one hand over the edge of the hole. It was a tight fit. He moved his foot up and pushed again, turning sideways to get his shoulder through. Lexie gave a final tug, and he tumbled out onto the grassy bank of a hill.

Chapter Six
ESCAPING MARSH ISLAND

Jake sucked in the fresh air. It felt good to be out of the cave. Out of the dark. And away from the horrible smell of the bats.

"What do we do now?" said Tommy, looking around as if he expected someone to come out of the trees and take them home.

"We head for the beach," said Lexie.

"Yeah," Jake agreed. "There might be someone camping down there." *Or there might not*, he thought to himself. It was autumn. Camping season was almost over. It was possible there was no one on the island but them.

Jake and Lexie put their arms under Tommy's, helping him down the hill to the woods. It was dark and cool in the woods. The ground squelched under their wet shoes. Jake knew the beach and the campsite were on the opposite side of the island. It was a long way. They had to go through bushes and groves of trees and around rock faces too steep to climb over.

For once, Lexie didn't have anything useful in her pockets to help them. A compass would have been good. Jake kept an eye on the position of the sun, crossed his fingers and hoped they were going in the right direction.

They hobbled up rises and down slopes, across a small ridge and through dense forest. The trees all looked the same.

Jake was beginning to think they were lost when he spotted a shimmer of light up ahead.

"I told you we were going the right way," he said, pointing. "There's the stream."

Finding the creek renewed their energy. They hurried downstream, half dragging, half carrying Tommy. At last they neared the campsite.

"Hello!" Jake called.

"Is anyone there?" said Lexie.

Breaking through the bushes, they stumbled into the campsite. It was empty.

Tommy slumped onto a tree stump. "No one's here," he said. "We're stuck here forever. No one's ever gonna find us."

"Of course someone will find us," said Jake. "Let's go check the beach." He heard a rumble in the distance. His head jerked up. "Do you hear that? It's a boat," he said.

"There's someone at the beach!" Lexie said.

Jake raced down the path toward the ocean. It wasn't far, but it seemed to take forever. As his feet hit the sand, he saw a small motorboat pulling away from shore.

"Hey! Wait! Wait for us!" Jake said, racing toward the water's edge.

The man had his back to Jake. He didn't see him. And he couldn't hear him over the noise of the outboard motor.

"Hey! Wait!" Jake screamed.

The boat was pulling away, dipping up and down in the surf.

Jake dashed into the water. "Waaaiiiiit!" But the man didn't turn around.

A whistle pierced the air. Lexie ran up beside Jake. She stuck her fingers in her mouth and whistled again, long and high.

The man turned to look in their direction.

"Wait for us!" Jake said, waving his arms madly.

"Come back!" Lexie shouted.

The man slowed the boat and turned back toward the beach. It was Chris Mumford, from the Marsh Island Historical Society.

"He's coming back," Tommy said, limping up behind them. "We're saved!"

Jake watched as the boat approached. He felt drained and weak.

"We did it," Lexie said. She thumped Jake on the back so hard he stumbled forward and almost fell in the water.

Jake grinned at her. "Yeah. We did."

As they waited for the boat, Tommy leaned over to Jake. "Does this mean we won the race?" he asked.

Jake stared at Tommy. After everything that had happened, he'd forgotten about the race.

"We got to Smuggler's Cave first, right?" said Tommy. "We won." He looked up at Jake eagerly.

"Yeah, Tommy. We won the race," said Jake, with a smug grin at Lexie.

Lexie stuck her tongue out at him.

"That's good," said Tommy and he smiled.

Jake laughed and ruffled Tommy's hair. Little brothers could be such a pain.

Sonya Spreen Bates was born in the United States but moved to Victoria, British Columbia, when she was very young. She began writing children's fiction in 2001, inspired by her two daughters and their love of the stories she told them.

She is the author of *Marsh Island* (Orca Book Publishers), *A Tank of Trouble* (Scholastic Education Australia) and *Midnight Ghost* (Limelight Press). Her short stories have been published in school magazines in Australia and New Zealand. *Smuggler's Cave* is her second book with Orca. She currently lives in Adelaide, Australia.